ANDREW'S LOOSE TOOTH

by Robert Munsch

Illustrated by Michael Martchenko

SCHOLASTIC INC. Cartwheel BOOKS®

New York Toronto London Auckland Sydney
Mexico City New Delhi Hong Kong Buenos Aires

Illustrations in this book were painted in watercolor
on Crescent Illustration Board.

This book was designed in QuarkXPress,
with type set in 18 point Hiroshige Medium.

Text copyright © 1998 by Bob Munsch Enterprises, Ltd.
Illustrations copyright © 1998 by Michael Martchenko.
All rights reserved. Published by Scholastic Inc.
SCHOLASTIC, CARTWHEEL BOOKS, and associated logos are trademarks and/or registered trademarks of Scholastic Inc.

Library of Congress Cataloging-in-Publication Data available

ISBN 0-439-38850-3

17 16   9/0

Printed in the U.S.A.   23

This edition first printing, April 2002

For Andrew Munsch,
Guelph, Ontario
—R. M.

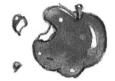

When Andrew came downstairs, there were three big red apples in the middle of the table. And even though he had a loose tooth, he decided to eat an apple.

So he reached out,
picked up an apple,
shined it on his shirt,
took a bite,
and yelled, "YEEE-OW! Mommy, Mommy! Do something about this tooth. It hurts so much I can't even eat my apple."

Andrew's mother opened up his mouth and looked inside.

"Ooh, ooh, ooh!" she said. "It's a loose tooth! I know what to do."

She took hold of the tooth with both hands and pulled as hard as she could. But the tooth did not come out.

"Oh, Andrew," she said, "I just can't get that tooth out. Why don't you try another apple? That might make your tooth come out."

So Andrew reached out,
picked up an apple,
shined it on his shirt,
took a bite,
and yelled, "YEEE-OW!
Daddy, Daddy! Do something about this tooth. It hurts so much I can't even eat my apple."

So Andrew's father opened up his mouth and looked inside.

"Ooh, ooh, ooh!" he said. "It's a loose tooth! I know what to do."

He got a big pair of pliers and took hold of Andrew's tooth. Then he put his foot on Andrew's nose and pulled as hard as he could. But the tooth did not come out.

"Oh, Andrew," he said, "this tooth is stuck. Why don't you try another apple? That will make your tooth come out."

So Andrew reached out,
picked up an apple,
shined it on his shirt,
took a bite,
and yelled, "**YEEE-OW!**
Mommy, Daddy, Mommy, Daddy! Do
something about this tooth. It hurts so
much I can't even eat my apple."
So they called a dentist.

The dentist came in a shiny black car. He opened up Andrew's mouth, looked inside and said, "Ooh, ooh, ooh! It's a loose tooth! I know what to do."

He got a big, long rope and he tied one end to Andrew's tooth.

Andrew said, "I know what you're going to do! I know what you're going to do! You're going to tie the end of the rope to the door and then you're going to slam the door!"

"NO!" said the dentist. "I'm going to tie it to my car."

He tied the other end of the rope to his car and drove away as fast as he could. When he got to the end of the rope, his whole car fell apart. The dentist stood there holding just the steering wheel.

Then Andrew's mother and his father and the dentist all said, "Andrew, Andrew. That tooth will not come out. You just can't eat your breakfast."

Andrew sat out in the front yard looking very sad. His best friend, Louis, came along and said, "Andrew, what's the matter?"

"Oh," said Andrew, "my mother can't get this tooth out. My father can't get this tooth out. The dentist can't get this tooth out. And I can't eat my breakfast."

"Ooh, ooh, ooh!" said Louis. "I know what to do."

Louis went into Andrew's house and called the Tooth Fairy on the phone. The Tooth Fairy roared up right away on a large motorcycle.

Andrew looked at the Tooth Fairy and said, "If you think you are going to use that motorcycle to pull out my tooth, you are nuts."

"What do you think I am?" said the Tooth Fairy. "A dentist?"

She pulled Andrew's tooth with one hand and the tooth did not come out.

She pulled Andrew's tooth with two hands and the tooth did not come out.

She got a large hammer off her motorcycle and clanged Andrew's loose tooth. The hammer broke in two pieces, and the tooth still did not come out.

"Incredible," said the Tooth Fairy. "This is the first tooth ever that I can't pull out. I guess you just can't eat your breakfast!"

"Hold it," said Louis, "I have an idea."

Louis went into Andrew's house and got a pepper shaker. Then he pushed back Andrew's head and sprinkled pepper up Andrew's nose.

Andrew went,

"Ah, ahhh,
Ah, Ahhhh,

AHHHHH-CHOO!"

. . . and sneezed that tooth all the way across town.

But the Tooth Fairy still got her tooth.